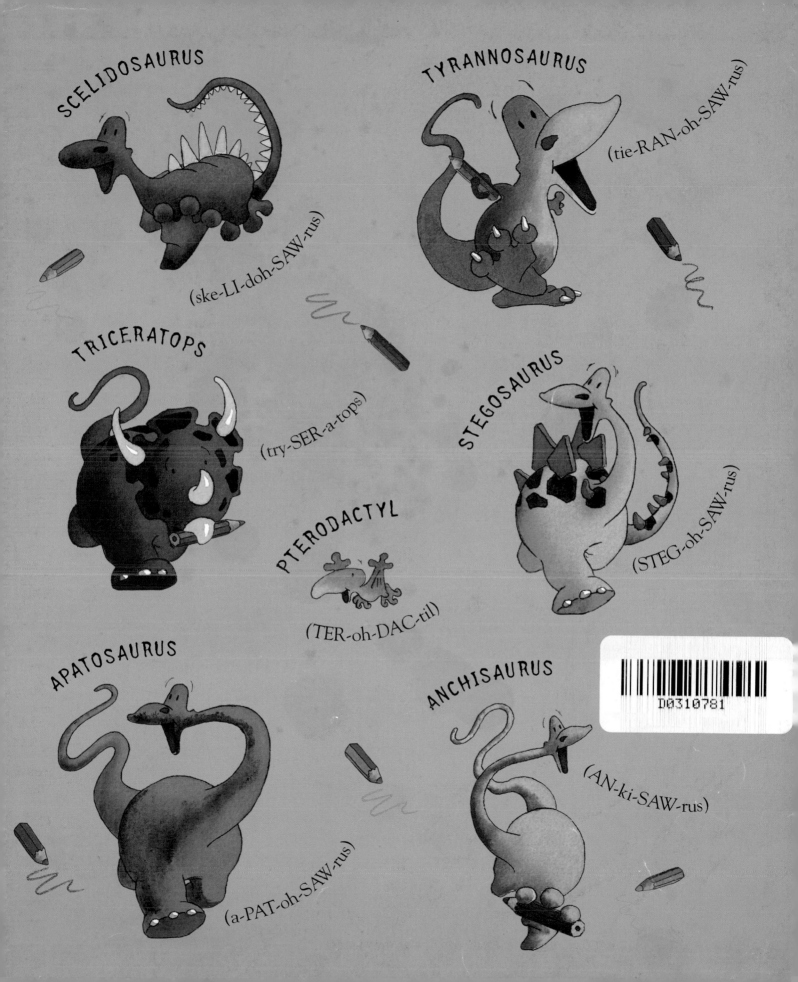

SCELIDOSAURUS

(ske-LI-doh-SAW-rus)

TYRANNOSAURUS

(tie-RAN-oh-SAW-rus)

TRICERATOPS

(try-SER-a-tops)

PTERODACTYL

(TER-oh-DAC-til)

STEGOSAURUS

(STEG-oh-SAW-rus)

APATOSAURUS

(a-PAT-oh-SAW-rus)

ANCHISAURUS

(AN-ki-SAW-rus)

In memory of Mason Jones and for all of his friends
at Deri Primary School, Bargoed, who miss him very much - I.W.

For Calum - A.R.

PUFFIN BOOKS
Published by the Penguin Group: London, New York, Ireland, Australia, Canada, India, New Zealand and South Africa
Penguin Books Ltd, Registered Offices: 80 Strand, London WC2R 0RL, England

www.penguin.com

Published in Puffin Books 2006
3 5 7 9 10 8 6 4 2
Text copyright © Ian Whybrow, 2006
Illustrations copyright © Adrian Reynolds, 2006
All rights reserved
The moral right of the author and illustrator has been asserted
Manufactured in China
ISBN-13: 978–0–141–38121–3
ISBN-10: 0–141–38121–3

Harry and the Dinosaurs Go To School

Ian Whybrow and Adrian Reynolds

PUFFIN

It was a big day for Harry. He was starting at his new school.
He was very excited because one of his friends, Charlie,
was starting that day too.

Stegosaurus said he didn't want to go. Not after
Triceratops told him about no Raaahs in class.
Mum said not to worry, school would be fine.

Harry blew his whistle just like a teacher.
   He said, "In twos, holding hands, my dinosaurs.
No talking and jump in the bucket."

The dinosaurs did what Harry said.
   All except Stegosaurus. He was so
nervous, all his plates were rattling.
   Harry had to give him a special stroke.

Sam said, "You can't take dinosaurs to school, stupid!"
That's why her toast fell on the floor.

Mum took Harry to school.

Mrs Rance was waiting at the classroom door when
Harry and Mum got there.
  "Hello, Harry," she said. "Welcome to your new school."
They all said goodbye to the mums and dads.

Then Mrs Rance showed Harry the coat pegs.
"You can leave your lunchbox here too," she said.
Harry was too shy to say could he have his bucket back.
That's why his dinosaurs got left outside the classroom.

Harry missed his dinosaurs, so he didn't like the classroom.
He didn't like the home corner, or his special work tray.

And he felt sorry for another new boy with a digger
who cried when his mum went home.
The boy wouldn't say one single word, not even his name.

Harry sort of liked the playground at playtime.
But it wasn't much fun, even the monkey bars –
not without his dinosaurs.

Back in class, the digger boy still wouldn't speak.
   "Maybe he wants to go to the toilet," Harry suggested.
"I'll show him where it is, shall I?"
   Mrs Rance said good idea, how thoughtful.

All the way to the toilet the boy kept quiet.
  It was the same on the way back, till they got to the coats.
Then they heard a voice, very sad and very soft.
  "Raaaaaaaaaaah!" it said.

"That's my dinosaurs," said Harry. "They miss me. Would you like to see them?"

The boy nodded so Harry said, "This is my Apatosaurus and my Anchisaurus and my Scelidosaurus.

This is Triceratops and Tyrannosaurus. Pterodactyl is the baby.
Wait! Where's Stegosaurus?"

"Jump out, Stegosaurus," called Harry. "Don't be shy!"

But Stegosaurus wanted a whisper.

"Ah," said Harry. "Stegosaurus says he will come out but only if he can have a ride on your digger."

And do you know what? The boy nodded and passed it over.

When Harry and the boy got back, Mrs Rance said,
"Oh good! Dinosaurs. I love dinosaurs. Do they Raaah?"

"RAAAAAAAAAAAAAH!" said the dinosaurs
and blew all the windows open.
   "My goodness!" said Mrs Rance. "That *was* a Raaah!"

They all sat down in the classroom.
  "Now, we're going to make new labels for our
coat pegs," said Mrs Rance. "Hands up who knows
how to write their name?"

The boy with the digger put up his hand.
  "And what are you going to write?" smiled Mrs Rance.
  "Jackosaurus!" said the boy.
  It was the very first word he had spoken all day.
And what a good joke, too!
  All the other children laughed and laughed.

Harry felt very happy.
   Charlie, Harry and their new friend Jack sat down together at a table with the dinosaurs.

They laughed and they Raaahed
and they made beautiful labels
to show where they belonged.

ENDOSAURUS

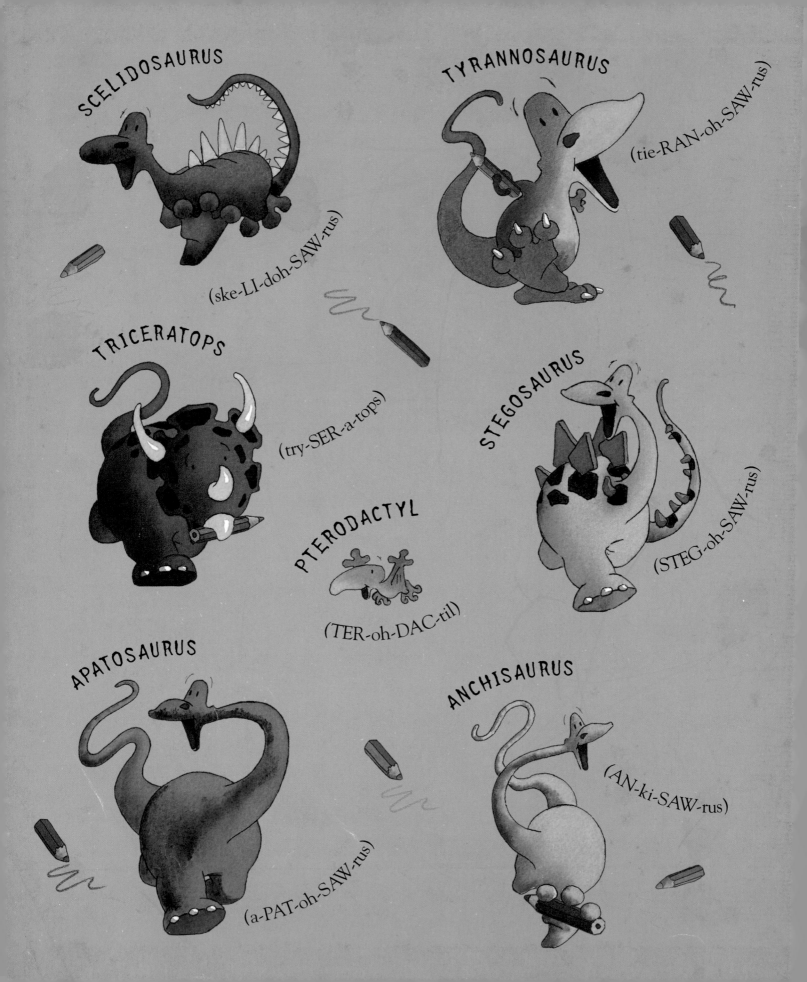